TO

RILEY

LOVE FROM

....

Riley has a pet unlike any other. He doesn't have whiskers, or fur, or cute fluffy ears.

He doesn't fetch sticks in the park, or chase his tail, and he can't curl up in Riley's lap for a snooze.

But he does have three LITTLE toes.

And a L-O-N-G neck.

And an even L-O-N-G-E-R tail.

And that's because Riley's pet is a dinosaur.

Called Dexter.

Although Dexter can't meow, or bark, or squeak, or moo, or quack, he does have a great big roar. Just not today.

"It's … gone," whispered Dexter. "Yesterday I was roaring loads, but now there's nothing. Not even a growl."

"It can't have vanished completely," said Riley. "We'll just have to look for it. Come on, let's go!"

And so their great roar hunt began….

First, Riley and Dexter searched the park. As they walked around, Riley thought he could hear something. Could it really be Dexter's roar?

OOMPAH! OOMPAH! OOMPAH!

"That's not my roar, that's a brass band!" said Dexter.

"Carry on walking down the road," said the band leader. "I'm sure I heard something earlier today that could have been a roar."

"Thanks!" said Riley. "Let's go, Dexter!"

Suddenly, Riley and Dexter heard a booming sound that got louder and louder.

But the closer and closer they got, the less and less it sounded like a roar.

BOOM! BOOM! BOOM!

Riley turned to Dexter: "That's not …"

"… my roar," frowned Dexter.

"Ha! My wrecking ball's never been mistaken for a dinosaur roar before," chuckled the crane driver. "Try the beach, there's always strange noises coming from there."

"Phew," said Riley. "All this roar hunting is tiring work. Come on, let's get an ice cream."

As Riley and Dexter wandered across the sand they heard a distant sound getting closer.

"Uh-oh, what's that?" said Dexter.

SQUAWK! SQUAWK! SQUAWK!

"Aaahh! Seagulls!" shouted Riley. "They're after the ice cream! Time for more roar hunting!"

They ran and ran and ran until they could run no more.

Suddenly, Dexter spotted something big, red and shiny coming towards them. It was their friendly neighbourhood firefighters.

"Hey, our siren can make a noise as big as a roar," they said. "Will that do?"

NEE-NAW! NEE-NAW! NEE-NAW!

"Hmm, it's kind of close, but it's still not really a roar," said Riley.

"It's a nee-no from me," said Dexter.

"Why don't you try asking a vet why your roar's disappeared?" said the firefighters. "We'll take you to see our friend — hop in!"

"I've never ever examined a dinosaur before," said the vet. "Oh well, here goes!"

"AAAHHH," said Dexter as she looked down his throat.

"EEEEK," said Dexter as she looked in his ears.

"WAA, that tickles," said Dexter as she examined his tummy.

"Well, this is strange, I can't see anything," puzzled the vet. "Why don't you go to the school library and hunt for your roar there?"

BRRRRIIINNGGG

SCHOOL

Riley spotted his best friend's brother in the playground.

"Dinosaur books?" he said. "Yes, there's loads in the library. Go in the main door and just follow the signs."

"Come on, Dexter, let's go!" said Riley.

"WHAT?" shouted Dexter.

"The library!" explained Riley.

"WHAT?!" yelled Dexter.

"Unblock your ears, Dexter!" said Riley.

"WHAT?!?" bellowed Dexter.

And so the great roar hunt continued as they tiptoed into the library, trying their best not to be heard.

Riley glanced back. "Whatever you do, Dexter, don't ..."
CLONK! "... hit your head on the light shade. Or ..."

THUMP! THUMP! THUMP!

"... knock any books off the shelves. Or ..." *SSHHHH!*
"... upset the librarian."

Riley sighed. "Are you sure you're not a clumsy-saurus?!"

They quickly found a comfy spot and started flicking through the dinosaur books.

"Any luck?" asked Riley.

"Not yet," replied Dexter. "Oh wait, look!"

Riley peeked round excitedly.

"I think that's a picture of my Uncle Dave in this one!" chuckled Dexter.

Book after book, page after page, they hunted and hunted until Riley noticed a big blue book tucked away in the corner.

"Hang on, that one's wobbling," said Riley.

"What. Is. That?" said Dexter.

Riley took a deep breath and opened it up. A ginormous roar erupted from the pages and whooshed into Dexter's mouth.

"RRRROOOOOAAAAAARRRR!"

"YAAAAYYYY!" cheered Riley.

"SHHHHHHH!" hissed the librarian.

"ROAR," whispered Dexter happily.

After a long day of brass band listening, seagull dodging, fire engine riding, puppy playing, library tiptoeing, head clonking and roar finding, Riley and Dexter headed back home.

"What a roar-some day!" they cheered.

"Yay for roars and dino-snores," thought Riley as he drifted off to sleep and began to dream of his next BIG adventure....

MEET SANTA?

EXPLORE SPACE?

Riley, look out for more **Mini Adventures** books.
Go to www.orangutanbooks.co.uk

Story by M.K. Scott
Illustrated by Jo Lindley
Designed by Ryan Dunn

orangutan

First published by Orangutan Books in 2019
Hometown World Ltd, 1 Queen Street, Bath BA1 1HE

Visit
www.orangutanbooks.co.uk
Follow us @orangutanbooks

MIX
Paper from
responsible sources
FSC® C023419